For Ruby and Phoebe Graves,
who know all about teachers. S.M.
For Tom. T.M.

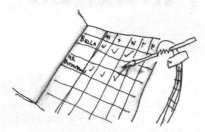

ORCHARD BOOKS
96 Leonard Street, London EC2A 4XD
Orchard Books Australia
32/45-51 Huntley Street, Alexandria, NSW 2015
ISBN 1 84362 564 4 (hardback)
ISBN 1 84362 572 5 (paperback)
First published in Great Britain in 2005
First paperback publication in 2006
Text © Sue Mongredien 2005
Illustrations © Teresa Murfin 2005
The rights of Sue Mongredien to be identified as the author
and of Teresa Murfin to be identified as the illustrator of this work
have been asserted by them in accordance with the
Copyright, Designs and Patents Act, 1988.
A CIP catalogue record for this book is available
from the British Library.
1 3 5 7 9 10 8 6 4 2 (hardback)
1 3 5 7 9 10 8 6 4 2 (paperback)
Printed in Great Britain
www.wattspublishing.co.uk

HEADMASTER DISASTER

SUE MONGREDIEN • TERESA MURFIN

ORCHARD BOOKS

Bella Boffinbrain hated school. It wasn't because she was unpopular. She had fabulous friends.

It wasn't because she was stupid. She did well in all her lessons.

It wasn't even anything to do with the teachers. Most of them were OK.

The big problem was the headmaster. He was strict and serious and bossy.

Worst of all, he was Bella's dad, too.

Unlike his daughter, Mr Boffinbrain looked forward to school every morning. He relished writing up rules and rotas and he loved long assemblies. In fact, he liked his headmasterly duties so much, he couldn't stop them, even when he was at home.

At the breakfast table every day, he would call a register. "Good morning, household," he would say. "Bella Boffinbrain?"

"Yes, Dad," Bella would sigh. "I'm here, as always, on the other side of the cereal packet."

"And I'm here, as well," Mr Boffinbrain would say, ticking off both of their names. "So we're all present and correct. Jolly good."

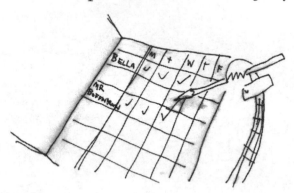

As well as their breakfast register, there was a homework hour every evening.

8

There was a 'Headmaster's Hundred' quiz every Friday night.

There was a weekly fire drill, which always came at the worst possible moments.

And if Bella ever did anything wrong, she was given lines as a punishment. *I must not tape over Dad's Open University videos with soap operas,* she'd have to write out fifty times.

I must not decorate Dad's dinner ladies' rota with flowers.

I must not put smiley face stickers on Dad's briefcase...

Of course, it hadn't always been like this. Bella's earliest memories were of growing up in the circus with her glamorous acrobat mum, and her daredevil, trapeze-artist dad. Davie Dare, he'd been called in those days.

But one day, a motorbike stunt went
terribly wrong, and Bella's mum died. Bella's
dad was so broken-hearted, he and Bella left
the circus at once.

No more danger, he vowed. He retrained as a teacher instead, and changed his surname from Dare to Boffinbrain. Somehow it seemed more fitting.

And that had been that. No more
dangling from high wires by his ankles.

No more twisting himself into
bone-bendingly impossible contortions.

After several years' hard work, Mr
Boffinbrain became a devoted headmaster.

"I think I'm going to start calling myself something else," Bella moaned to her best friend, Lucy, one Monday morning. "I'm sick of people thinking I must be a geek, just because I'm a Boffinbrain."

Before Lucy could reply, Mr Boffinbrain came to the front of the assembly hall, and clapped his hands for quiet.

"Good morning, girls and boys," he said.

"Good morning, Mr Boffinbrain," the school droned in reply.

"Now then," Mr Boffinbrain said, "before our first song, I've got an urgent request for new playground litter collectors. Hands up who wants to join my litter patrol team!"

Not a single hand moved. Every child in the hall could think of far better things to do at breaktimes than picking up empty crisp packets and sticky drink cartons.

Mr Boffinbrain's bushy eyebrows sank into a frown. "No one?"

A deathly hush
settled over the hall.
For once in her life,
Felicity "the fidget"
Foster sat
perfectly still.

Millie "the mouth"
Masters clamped her
lips shut.

Even Alastair
"ants in his pants"
Andrews seemed
frozen to the spot.

Bella held her breath and wished she could make herself invisible. She knew exactly what was coming next...

"Very well. Bella, you can help me," said Mr Boffinbrain. "Leo Webster, you too. Come to my office at break. Together we will wage war on the litter louts!"

"Oh, *Da-a-ad*," Bella groaned without thinking. The rest of her class tittered loudly around her. Leo Webster shot Bella a dirty look, as if it was all her fault.

"Great," sighed Bella. Now Leo Webster hated her, on top of everything else. Thanks, Dad. Thanks for *nothing*!

After a long lunch hour spent chasing after sweet wrappers with her dad and Leo, Bella was in a bad mood. She was sick of always being roped in to do the jobs nobody else wanted to do, like cleaning smelly gerbil cages, or sorting piles of football kit. It was time for action.

And so, at the tea table that evening, Bella cleared her throat. "Dad," she said, "I—"

DING-DONG!

Mr Boffinbrain put his fork down crossly. "Really!" he said. "Six o'clock is tea-time. Who can that be?"

"I'll go," said Bella.

DING-DONG!

On the doorstep stood a woman with leopard-print trousers, a gold sequinned jacket and big hair. As soon as she saw Bella, she clapped a manicured hand to her mouth. "If it isn't little Bella!" she cried. "Aren't you a sweetheart? The very image of your mum!"

Bella stared at this woman who seemed as loud and colourful as an exotic bird. "Er..." she said hesitantly. "Who are you? Do you know my dad?"

"Know him? I used to dangle from his elbows, sweetie!" the woman exclaimed. "Mitzi Bitzi, pleased to meet you again. I'm from the circus. I used to push you around in your pram when you were just a tot!"

"You'd better come in," Bella said, trying hard to imagine Mitzi swinging from a trapeze with her dad. "Dad," she called, as Mitzi click-clacked her way inside. "You've got a visitor."

Mitzi bustled ahead. "Where's my little chucky-chops? I've been so excited about seeing... Ooh! Here he is!"

With a blur of colour and a volley of squeals, she threw herself at Bella's dad, and kissed his cheeks. "Davie Dare, how do you DO?" she cried. "Remember me? Little old itsy-bitsy Mitzi Bitzi?"

Mr Boffinbrain's face was a picture. A picture of shock, first of all. But then his frozen, stunned expression slowly melted and gave way to a smile. "Well, I *never*!" he chortled. "Mitzi Bitzi! How are you?"

"Me? Oh, I'm just marvellous," she said, her eyes twinkling. "Marvellous and...well, homeless, actually," she sighed. "So I was wondering if you could put me up? Just until I find somewhere else to live?"

Having Mitzi Bitzi in the Boffinbrain house was like a breath of fresh air. Homework hour was forgotten as Mitzi entertained them with gossip and funny stories about all their old circus pals.

The 'Headmaster's Hundred' became 'Mitzi's Fifty' where they had to think up fifty jokes between them.

Best of all were the stories that Mitzi told Bella about her father as a trapeze artist. "He would soar through the air like a glittering blue eagle," she would tell Bella. "All the ladies would come to see your father. Davie Dare was the star turn of the circus! Your mum was so proud. Such a shame that he walked away from it all."

"I don't remember him ever being like that," Bella confessed sadly. "He's so sensible these days."

Mitzi nodded. "He is, isn't he?" she mused. Then she elbowed Bella and gave her another one of her winks. "We'll soon sort that out, love. Don't you worry!"

By the end of the week, Bella was starting to think Mitzi was right. If anybody could liven up David Boffinbrain, it was Mitzi with her cheeky jokes and shrieks of laughter. Within days, Dad had started talking fondly about life in the circus.

So far, so good. But then came Bella's friend Lucy's birthday party on Saturday. She was having a bowling party, followed by a birthday tea of burgers, chips and knickerbocker glories. In other words, the perfect afternoon. Only, it wasn't.

The party started off fine. Lucy had invited
nine other girls and soon they were all having
fantastic fun, flinging bowling balls down
the lanes.

It wasn't until they began the party tea that Bella had a bad feeling. As soon as Lucy's mum and dad had gone up to the counter to pay for the food, she heard a familiar-sounding voice. "Hey, look, everyone, it's baby Boffin!"

Bella turned around, cheeks burning, to see
Leo Webster and his gang.

"Daddy Boffin let you off the litter patrol,
did he?" sneered Leo. Then he pointed at an
old chip box on the floor. "Quick, litter
leader, better wage war on that rubbish!"

"Get lost, Leo," Lucy told him. "Leave her alone."

"Well, she'd better tell darling Daddy to leave *me* alone then," Leo said. "If I end up on that stupid litter patrol *again*, I'll..."

"WEBSTER! I hope you're not threatening my daughter!"

Bella shut her eyes in dismay and put her head on the table. Oh, no. Please let this all be a bad dream!

"As if I'd threaten Bella, Mr B," Leo said.

"Good," said Mr Boffinbrain. "Clear off, then. Leave these girls to their glorious knickers."

"Knickerbocker *glories*, Dave," she heard Mitzi say, while everyone on the table burst out laughing.

glorious knickers

"Jolly good. Whatever you say," Mr
Boffinbrain replied. "Right, Bella. Had a
super time? Ready to go?"

"Dad, you're early. We're still eating,"
Bella hissed. "Can't you wait outside or
something, like normal parents?"

Mitzi gave her a sympathetic look. "I did tell him, love, but you know what he's like," she clucked. Then she lowered her voice. "He was the same in the circus. Very headstrong. Very dynamic."

Now it was Mr Boffinbrain's turn to be embarrassed. Red in the face, he strode off towards the exit. Mitzi ran after him.

Bella coughed, feeling like the biggest idiot in the universe. "Sorry about that, everyone," she said. "Er...what were we talking about?"

"Did she say *circus*?" Lucy asked.

"Was Mr B in the *circus*?" Jasmine wanted to know.

Bella sighed. "Do you mind if we talk about something else?" she asked. "I kind of want to forget all that just happened."

Meanwhile, Mr Boffinbrain and Mitzi were just walking past the Megabowl kitchen on their way outside when...KA-BOOM!

"Help!" screamed a voice. "Fire!"

Everyone in the Megabowl stared at the wall of flame that had shot up in the kitchen.

Then came a commanding shout from Mr Boffinbrain. "Fire drill! At once! Evacuate the building!"

Nobody needed telling twice. There was a mad stampede for the exit.

"Quickly but calmly," barked Mr Boffinbrain. "Has anybody got any water?"

Somebody threw a bottle of mineral water at him, and he caught it, then ripped off his jumper and started soaking it. Bella and her friends were outside now, watching through the window.

"What's he *doing*?" breathed Jasmine, her eyes goggling.

The fire was blazing so fiercely, nobody wanted to get near it. Mr Boffinbrain, however, took a running jump and launched himself up into the air. He clung onto the overhead light and soared across the ceiling so that he was above all the flames.

The crowd outside the window stared as he nimbly hooked his feet around the light cable and swung upside down, arms outstretched, holding the wet jumper between his teeth.

"Look at him go," marvelled Lucy. "He really was in the circus, wasn't he?"

Lucy's mum had turned pink. "It's Davie Dare," she cried, nudging her husband. "I always wondered what happened to him!"

A hush fell over the crowd outside as Mitzi leapt up towards Mr Boffinbrain. He caught hold of her free hand, and they swung together for a second, while everyone watching held their breath. They were right above the start of the blaze now.

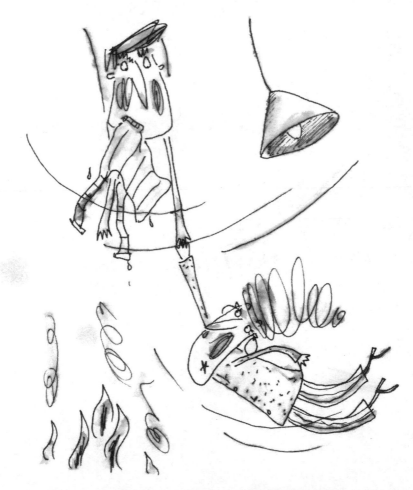

Mitzi took the wet jumper from Mr Boffinbrain's mouth, then turned upside down so that he was holding her by the ankles. Then they swung together towards the fire and Mitzi dropped the wet jumper right on top of the source of the flames.

PSSSSSSSHHHHHHHHHHHHHHHHHHH!
Bella stood on tiptoes to get a better view.
"The fire's out!" she cried proudly. "They've
done it!"

Mitzi performed a perfect back flip landing. Then Mr Boffinbrain dropped gracefully to the floor beside her..

A thunderous roar of applause echoed around the bowling alleys, as everyone ran inside again, cheering their heads off. Mr Boffinbrain and Mitzi were mobbed by bowlers and staff.

Bella's friends danced around, whooping with excitement. The chefs ran out from the kitchen to kiss Mitzi and throw their arms around Mr Boffinbrain.

"Wow," Bella heard Leo Webster say admiringly. "I never knew the old Boff had it in him."

From then on, everything changed. Mr Boffinbrain and Mitzi were heroes. They appeared on the front page of all the local newspapers and were interviewed on the local radio station.

The news spread around the school, too,
and suddenly everyone thought their
headmaster was the coolest man alive. Mitzi
even persuaded Mr Boffinbrain to start circus
skill workshops in the school holidays which
were wildly popular.

Did I say that *everything* changed...? Not quite. Mr Boffinbrain still insisted on Bella's homework hour in the evening. He still arranged the occasional fire drill at home.

And he still took a breakfast register every morning, but there was a slight change to that. "Good morning, household," Mr Boffinbrain would say at the kitchen table. "Bella Boffinbrain?"

"Yes, Dad," Bella would sigh. "I'm here, as always, on the other side of the cereal packet."

"And...er..." Mr Boffinbrain would say, with a shy smile, "*Mrs* Boffinbrain?"

"Yes, chucky-chops," Mitzi would reply, with a wink. "I'm here, too."

"And I am, as well," Mr Boffinbrain would say, ticking off their names. "So we're all present and correct. Jolly good."

Then he would lean over the table and kiss his new wife. Bella would always roll her eyes and pretend to be sick, but secretly she liked it. In fact, she thought it was jolly good, too.

FRIGHTFUL FAMILIES

WRITTEN BY SUE MONGREDIEN • ILLUSTRATED BY TERESA MURFIN

Explorer Trauma	1 84362 571 7
Headmaster Disaster	1 84362 572 5
Millionaire Mayhem	1 84362 573 3
Clown Calamity	1 84362 574 1
Popstar Panic	1 84362 575 X
Football-mad Dad	1 84362 576 8
Chef Shocker	1 84362 577 6
Astronerds	1 84362 803 1

All priced at £3.99

Frightful Families are available from all good book shops, or can be ordered direct from the publisher: Orchard Books, PO BOX 29, Douglas IM99 1BQ
Credit card orders please telephone 01624 836000
or fax 01624 837033 or visit our Internet site: www.wattspub.co.uk
or e-mail: bookshop@enterprise.net for details.

To order please quote title, author and ISBN
and your full name and address.
Cheques and postal orders should be made payable to 'Bookpost plc.'
Postage and packing is FREE within the UK
(overseas customers should add £1.00 per book).
Prices and availability are subject to change.